The Music Fairies

Special thanks to
Narinder Dhami

ORCHARD BOOKS
338 Euston Road, London NW1 3BH
Orchard Books Australia
Level 17/207 Kent Street, Sydney, NSW 2000
A Paperback Original

First published in 2008 by Orchard Books

HiT entertainment

A CIP catalogue record for this book is available
from the British Library.

ISBN 978 1 40830 033 6
3 5 7 9 10 8 6 4 2

Printed and bound in China by Imago

Orchard Books is a division of Hachette Children's Books,
an Hachette UK company

www.hachette.co.uk

Poppy
the Piano
Fairy

by Daisy Meadows

ORCHARD BOOKS

www.rainbowmagic.co.uk

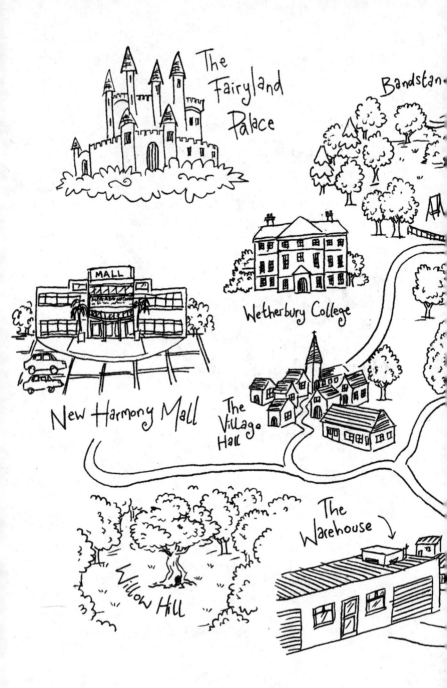

I'm through with frost, ice and snow.
To the human world I must go!
I'll form a cool, Gobolicious Band.
Magical instruments will lend a hand.

With these instruments I'll go far.
Frosty Jack, a superstar.
I'll steal music's harmony and fun.
Watch out world, I'll be number one!

Contents

A Musical Message

"Ooh, I love to dance!" Rachel Walker sang along to the radio, pretending her hairbrush was a microphone. "When I hear the music, my toes start tapping and my fingers start snapping – I just love to dance!"

Kirsty Tate, Rachel's best friend, grinned and grabbed her own hairbrush.

"I can't stop dancing!" she chorused. "Just can't stop dancing!"

The girls tried to do a complicated dance routine as they sang, but then Kirsty went left and Rachel went right and they ended up bumping into each other. Laughing, they collapsed onto Kirsty's bedroom carpet.

"It's really hard to sing and dance at the same time," said Rachel as the song ended.

"I know," Kirsty agreed. "I don't think we'd be very good in a band, Rachel!"

"That was The Sparkle Girls with their new single, *Can't Stop Dancing*", the radio DJ announced as Kirsty and Rachel sat up. "And if anyone out there thinks they could make it big as a pop star too, why not come along and audition for the National Talent Competition next weekend?"

Rachel and Kirsty glanced at each other.

"That sounds cool!" Rachel said.

"One lucky singer or band will win a recording contract with MegaBig Records," the DJ went on. "So remember – come along to the New Harmony Mall next weekend, and maybe one day I'll be playing *your* songs on my show!"

"The New Harmony Mall is only a few miles from Wetherbury," Kirsty said. "I'm sure Mum or Dad would take us to watch the competition if we asked them."

"That would be great," Rachel replied eagerly. "Isn't it lucky that the contest is taking place just before I go home?" Rachel was staying with Kirsty for the autumn half-term holiday, and her parents would be coming to collect her at the end of the following weekend.

"And now here's Leanne Roberts with her new song, *Magical Moments*," said the DJ.

"Oh, I love this one," Rachel remarked, turning the radio up a little.

"Me, too," Kirsty agreed. She smiled as Rachel began dancing round the room. "Maybe we should enter the Talent Competition ourselves!" Rachel laughed. "I'm a hopeless singer!" she said, pulling a face. "But I bet we'd have a lot of fun singing along with our friends in Fairyland, wouldn't we?"

Kirsty nodded. She and Rachel shared a very special and magical secret. They were good friends with the fairies and had visited Fairyland many times.

But the girls had never told anyone about their fairy adventures, not even their parents.

"Life is special, life is fun," Kirsty sang along to the radio as Rachel twirled around their beds. "Look for the magic in everyone!"

Then, very unexpectedly, the music changed. Kirsty and Rachel stared at each other in surprise as the bouncy tune of *Magical Moments* suddenly became a much sweeter and

softer melody. "Kirsty and Rachel!" a tiny, silvery voice sang from the radio. "Can you hear me, girls?"

Rachel and Kirsty could hardly believe their ears.

"There's a fairy speaking to us through the radio!" Kirsty gasped.

"Yes, we can hear you!" Rachel declared, breathless with excitement.

"Girls, I'm so glad you were listening to music because that meant I could contact you immediately!" the fairy said, sounding very relieved. "My name is Poppy the Piano Fairy, and I'm one of the seven Music Fairies."

"Hello, Poppy!" said Rachel.

"Is everything OK in Fairyland?" asked Kirsty.

15

"Oh, girls, we're in terrible trouble!" the fairy went on anxiously. "We need your help right away. At this very moment Jack Frost and his goblins are invading Fairyland's Royal School of Music!"

Rachel and Kirsty looked horrified. Jack Frost and his naughty goblin servants were always causing trouble in Fairyland, and the girls had often helped their fairy friends to outwit them and prevent them from making mischief.

"What's Jack Frost up to?" Rachel wanted to know.

16

"Well, the school's a very special place because it's where all the fairies come to learn music," Poppy explained. "And it's where we Music Fairies keep our Magical Musical Instruments. They're very important because they make music fun and harmonious in Fairyland and in your human world. We think Jack Frost wants to steal the Magical Musical Instruments, and we need help to stop him from getting his icy hands on them! Can you come to Fairyland immediately, girls?"

"Of course we can," Rachel declared.

"We'll be there in a flash!" Kirsty added.

"Thank you, girls," Poppy replied gratefully. "Please hurry!"

Instantly, the fairy's voice faded away. Rachel and Kirsty quickly opened the gold lockets the Weather Fairies had given them after one of their adventures together. They each carefully took a pinch of the glittering fairy dust inside,

and then sprinkled it over themselves. A whirl of sparkling rainbow colours surrounded the girls, and suddenly they felt themselves tumbling through the air. As they did so, they shrank smaller and smaller until they were fairy-sized.

"I just hope we're in time to stop Jack Frost!" Kirsty cried.

Music School Mayhem

A few moments later, the bright rainbow colours swirled away, and the girls found themselves outside a tall white house next to the Fairyland palace. There was a gold sign on the gate with "Royal School of Music" written on it in pink letters.

The wooden doors of the school were flung wide open, and as Rachel and Kirsty hurried over, a fairy rushed out to meet them. She looked very stylish in her black wide-legged trousers and pink shirt, with a trilby perched on top of her red corkscrew curls.

"Girls, you're here!" the fairy exclaimed, looking very relieved. "I'm Poppy the Piano Fairy."

"Where are Jack Frost and his goblins now?" Kirsty asked as Poppy ushered them inside the school.

"They're on their way to the practice room," Poppy explained quickly, "and

that's where we keep the Magical
Musical Instruments. We have to stop
them!" She zoomed off
up the winding spiral
staircase. "Follow
me, girls!"

Rachel and
Kirsty whizzed
after Poppy. At
the top of
the stairs, the
fairy stopped,
hovering in the
open doorway
of a large room.
As the girls caught up
with Poppy, they gasped
aloud at the scene of chaos
in front of them.

The practice room was a complete mess. Cupboards stood open, chairs and music stands had been overturned, and there were various musical instruments as well as sheet music scattered all over the floor. In the middle of the mayhem were seven goblins, one of them holding an ice wand.

They were standing around a tangled
heap of musical instruments, gazing
eagerly at them with wide, greedy eyes.
Unlike the others lying around the room,
these instruments glowed with a faint,
magical sparkle. Kirsty and Rachel could
see a piano amongst them.

"Those are our Magical Musical Instruments!" Poppy whispered in dismay.

As Poppy, Rachel and Kirsty raced into the room, the goblin with the wand waved it over the instruments. A shower of ice crystals burst out and immediately shrank all the instruments down until they were tiny. The goblins laughed and cheered.

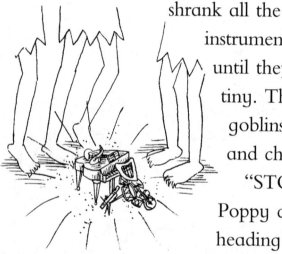

"STOP!" Poppy cried, heading towards them with Kirsty and Rachel close behind.

"Shan't!" the goblins jeered. They each grabbed one of the tiny instruments and dashed over to a window on the other side of the room.

"Ha ha ha!" laughed a familiar, icy voice. "The Magical Musical Instruments are mine!"

A cold shiver ran down Rachel's and Kirsty's spines as they saw that Jack Frost was waiting for the goblins by the open window.

Jack Frost saw the girls and scowled.

"You're too late, pesky human girls!" he shouted. "You won't stop me this time!"

He pointed his wand out of the
window and sent a freezing stream of icy
crystals shooting downwards. Within
seconds the crystals had formed an ice
slide. The goblins whooped with glee
and jumped onto the slide, still clutching
the tiny instruments. Then they zipped
smartly away down the slide as Poppy
and the girls watched on.

"Oh no!" Poppy gasped, "Jack
Frost and his goblins are
escaping with our Magical
Musical Instruments!"

"We can still stop them!" Rachel shouted in a determined voice.

The three friends dashed across the room towards the window, dodging overturned chairs and music stands. But as Jack Frost jumped onto the slide himself, he pointed his ice wand straight at them.

"Quick!" Poppy cried out in a panicked voice. "Hide!" She grabbed the girls' hands and pulled them behind a nearby drum set.

Kirsty's heart was pounding as she peeped around a drum, expecting to see one of Jack Frost's ice bolts come flying towards them.

But to her surprise, she saw a cloud of white paper stream from Jack Frost's wand and whirl around the room like confetti.

"How strange, It's just paper!" she shouted to Poppy and Rachel. "Hurry, Jack Frost is getting away!"

They all rushed out from behind the drum kit. But there was so much paper, it was like flying through a snowy blizzard. Poppy and the girls could hardly see where they were going. As they struggled over to the window, they could just see Jack Frost sliding off into the distance. And as he whizzed away in a storm of snowflakes, they could hear him chanting a spell:

"Goblins stand out because they're green,
But I don't want them to be seen.
I cast this spell so they'll blend in
And girls and fairies won't see them!"

"Whatever does that mean?" Kirsty asked, frowning. Meanwhile, Rachel began to climb onto the ice slide, but Poppy grabbed her arm.

"It's not safe, Rachel," the fairy said urgently. "Look, the ice is melting."

Rachel could see that Poppy was right.

"What are we going to do, then?" she asked anxiously. "We can't let Jack Frost

and his goblins get away with the instruments!"

"I must tell the other Music Fairies right away," Poppy sighed. "Maybe we can come up with a plan…"

Kirsty peered through the snowflakes spinning around outside the window. She could see the melting ice slide stretching far away into the distance. And right at the very end of the slide was something which looked very familiar. Kirsty frowned in concentration. Then suddenly she realised that the ice slide led to the bandstand in Wetherbury Park, not far from her house!

She was about to tell the others when
Rachel suddenly let out a huge gasp.
She'd picked up a handful of Jack Frost's
paper confetti and was
studying it more closely.

"This isn't confetti!"
she exclaimed. "The
sheets of paper are
tiny posters!"

Kirsty and Poppy
both picked up a
piece of confetti. Each poster had a
picture of Jack Frost, with some writing
underneath. Rachel read the words
aloud.

"'Jack Frost invites you to see Frosty
and his Gobolicious Band – appearing
in the human world as stars of the
National Talent Competition!'"

"Oh, that's what we heard on the radio, Rachel!" Kirsty gasped. "Jack Frost and his goblins are entering the competition – and if he wins, Jack Frost will be a star!"

"Oh, he'd like that, wouldn't he?" Rachel pointed out with a grin. "Jack Frost would love to have all the power and glory of being a pop star!"

Poppy was looking very worried indeed. "And unfortunately, with the help of our Magical Musical Instruments, Frosty and his Gobolicious Band are going to perform brilliantly!" she said sadly. "Jack Frost can't possibly lose – unless we can get our instruments back before the competition begins!"

Out of Tune

Rachel and Kirsty looked worried.

"If Jack Frost wins, there'll be a lot of publicity," Kirsty pointed out. "People will soon realise he's not human and then everyone will find out that fairies really do exist!"

"Yes, Fairyland will be discovered, and, with the Magical Musical Instruments stuck in the human world, music will be ruined for everyone, for ever!" Poppy replied, her wings drooping sadly.

Suddenly, six other fairies rushed in through the open door.

"We came as soon as we got your message, Poppy!" gasped one of them. "What happened?"

"Jack Frost got away with our Magical Musical Instruments," Poppy explained miserably, "even though Rachel, Kirsty and I did our best to stop him. He plans to enter the National Talent Competition in the human world!"

The other fairies gasped in horror.

"Girls, meet the Music Fairies," Poppy went on, turning to Rachel and Kirsty. "Ellie the Guitar Fairy, Fiona the Flute Fairy, Danni the Drums Fairy, Maya the Harp Fairy, Victoria the Violin Fairy and Sadie the Saxophone Fairy."

"Thank you for coming, girls," said Danni. "Will you help us get the instruments back?"

"Oh, please do!" Fiona chimed in. "We can't imagine life in Fairyland or the human world without music."

"Of course we'll help," Kirsty said, and Rachel nodded.

"We couldn't imagine life without music, either!"

"But where shall we start looking?" asked Sadie.

Suddenly Kirsty remembered what she'd seen at the end of the ice slide. "I know exactly where Jack Frost has gone," she cried. "His ice slide led to the bandstand in Wetherbury Park!"

"Well done, Kirsty!" Poppy declared. "Ellie, will you tell the king and queen about Jack Frost's latest mischief? I'll go with Rachel and Kirsty – they might need fairy magic to help them."

Ellie nodded. "And we'll clear up the school while you three find Jack Frost and his goblins." She pointed her wand at an overturned music stand and a shower of sparkles lifted it the right way up again. The other Music Fairies

joined in, their magic making the sheet music, chairs and instruments dance their way back to their proper places.

Meanwhile, Poppy waved her wand over herself and the girls, and her magic immediately whisked them off to Wetherbury in a mist of rainbow sparkles.

Just a moment later, the girls found themselves back to their normal size and standing in the park next to the bandstand.

"Any sign of Jack Frost and his goblins?" Poppy murmured, hovering out of sight behind Kirsty's hair.

The girls looked around. Everything seemed quite normal at first glance.

There was a man walking his dog, a couple of mothers with prams chatting on a nearby bench and a group of children playing on the swings.

But then Rachel noticed something rather strange. A young boy was standing looking at the bandstand wearing rather strange clothes. His bright yellow trousers were too long for him and his shirtsleeves were too short. He also wore a big, floppy, purple hat, which covered his face.

Rachel nudged Kirsty.

"Do you think that boy could be a goblin?" she whispered. "He's got a goblin's fashion sense!"

"Let's go and see," Kirsty replied.

Poppy and the girls went to take a closer look. But as they got nearer to the boy, Rachel shook her head.

"He can't be a goblin," she said. "Look at his arms – they're not green."

Poppy frowned. "I know my beautiful piano is close by, girls," she said. "I can feel its music calling to me. But where is it?"

"Maybe the goblins have left the park," Kirsty suggested.

"We could look in the High Street. There are plenty of places to hide there."

Poppy nodded and flew into Kirsty's pocket, out of sight. The girls then hurried towards the park gates. As they did so, they passed the mothers sitting on the bench. One of them was singing a lullaby to her baby, who was crying.

"Hush, little baby, go to sleep," she warbled in a voice that was horribly off-key.

Kirsty and Rachel exchanged worried looks as the baby began to cry even louder.

Then, just outside the park gates, they saw a busker playing the harmonica. But the tune sounded dreadful because the man simply couldn't hit any of the right notes. The result was a horrible screeching, ear-splitting noise.

"That's awful!" Rachel whispered to Kirsty, pulling a face as they passed by.

"I've seen that man busking here before, and he's usually really good," Kirsty replied. "This is all because the Magical Musical Instruments are missing.

Music everywhere is being spoiled!"

"You're right!" Poppy exclaimed. "No one can sing or play instruments properly any more. We must find Jack Frost and his goblins and return the instruments to Fairyland!"

The High Street was near the park, and Rachel and Kirsty began popping into the shops and cafés, looking for goblins. As they searched, they heard just how music was being ruined everywhere.

"Listen to that background music," Kirsty whispered to Rachel as they looked

around the local bookshop. "It's terrible!"

Rachel nodded. "It sounds like someone wailing, not singing!" she replied.

"My MP3 player's not working," a teenage boy complained to his mum, pulling the headphones out of his ears.

"The car horns are honking off-key, too," Kirsty remarked as they went outside again.

"And the birds are singing out of tune!" Rachel pointed out.

The girls hurried on down the High Street, trying not to listen to the awful noises all around them. But suddenly they heard something else – a sweet, pure melody wafting towards them on the breeze.

"That's my piano!" Poppy gasped.

Goblin Surprise!

Immediately, Rachel and Kirsty headed straight towards the clear, beautiful sound of Poppy's piano.

"It's coming from this music store!" Kirsty announced breathlessly.

She and Rachel peered through the display window, expecting to spot a goblin. But to their surprise, they saw the strangely dressed boy from the park.

He was
sitting on
a stool in
front of
Poppy's
piano, playing
a very difficult
piece of classical
music.

"Look, my piano's full-size
again!" Poppy whispered, peeking out
of Kirsty's pocket. "Remember the wand
the goblins had at the school? Jack Frost
must have given them the power to
change the size of our instruments.
We can do that with our fairy magic,
but usually the goblins can't."

The boy's fingers were now flashing
across the keyboard in a blur. He

finished the piece with a flourish, swept off his floppy hat and stood up to take a bow.

Kirsty and Rachel stared at him in disbelief.

"He *is* a goblin!" Kirsty exclaimed, staring at the boy's pointy ears and nose.

"But he's not green!" Rachel said, looking puzzled. "Oh!" Suddenly her eyes opened wide. "Remember Jack Frost's spell?

"Goblins stand out because they're green,
But I don't want them to be seen.
I cast this spell so they'll blend in
And girls and fairies won't see them!"

Rachel grinned. "Jack Frost has made the goblins human-coloured!" she declared.

"But they do still look like goblins," Kirsty added. "They've still got pointy noses and big feet and huge ears, so the spell didn't work completely!"

"And he's got my piano!" Poppy said, staring longingly through the window. "How are we going to get it back?"

They all stared at the goblin, who was now flexing his fingers, ready to play another tune. "I have an idea," Rachel said slowly.

"Maybe we should use the goblin's disguise against him."

"How?" asked Kirsty.

"I can pretend to be a goblin too!" Rachel replied. "I'll tell him Jack Frost wants to see him, so he can promote him to lead singer of the Gobolicious Band!" She  peered through the shop window. "Kirsty, you hide behind those big speakers and I'll direct the goblin over to you."

"Then I'll think of a way to keep him occupied while Poppy magics her piano back to Fairyland," Kirsty finished. "Great idea!"

"And guess what?" Poppy said, her eyes twinkling. "I can make your nose and ears a bit bigger, Rachel, so that you look more like a goblin!"

Poppy immediately flew out of Kirsty's pocket and showered Rachel with fairy dust. Kirsty watched closely and could hardly believe her eyes when Rachel's nose began to grow to a long point. At the same time, Rachel's ears grew bigger

and bigger until at last she looked
remarkably like a human-coloured
goblin!

Piano Plan

"How do I look?" Rachel asked, peering at her reflection in the display window.

"Just like a goblin!" Kirsty replied. She grinned at Rachel and then hurried into the shop. Rachel and Poppy waited for a moment until Kirsty had hidden herself safely behind the tall speakers.

Then Poppy flew behind Rachel's hair and they went into the music store.

First Rachel checked that the shop assistants were busy with customers before she made her way over to the goblin. She knew she had to act quickly before Poppy's magic wore off, and her nose and ears shrank back to their normal size.

But as Rachel got closer to the goblin, he saw her coming. Frowning, he whipped a wand out of his pocket.

It's the wand the goblins used at the school! Rachel thought, alarmed.
I'd better stop him before he shrinks Poppy's piano again and runs off with it!
The goblin lifted the wand.

"Wait!" Rachel called. "I'm a goblin too!" she added in a low voice.

The goblin stared suspiciously at her.

"How do I know you're a goblin?" he asked.

"Look at our reflections," Rachel told him, bending over the shiny piano top. She was really glad that Poppy had altered her features with fairy magic! "We both look human, don't we?"

The goblin nodded, still suspicious.

"Well, you look human but you're actually a goblin," Rachel went on. "And I look human too, so I must be a goblin like you, right?"

The goblin looked very confused. Rachel hoped desperately that he wouldn't think too carefully about what

she'd just said, but she was relying on the fact that goblins weren't very clever!

"Right," the goblin agreed at last, and Rachel tried not to sigh with relief.

"We've got the same ears and the same nose. But…" He glanced disdainfully at Rachel's jeans and T-shirt. "My human clothes are much nicer than yours!"

"Oh, they're lovely and bright,"
Rachel assured him.

"Yes, I like the clothes, but my skin
is awfully plain," the goblin grumbled.
"I miss being green. Green is such a
beautiful colour!"

Rachel tried not
to smile.

"I miss being green
too," she replied.
"But you know the
Gobolicious Band
is entering the
National Talent
Competition? Well, Jack Frost
wants to see you right away.
I think he's planning to promote
you to lead singer!"

"Me?" Looking tremendously excited, the goblin bounced up and down on the piano stool. "He's right – I'd be a great lead singer! My good looks are wasted behind this piano!"

This time Rachel really had to bite her lip to stop herself from laughing.

"Jack Frost is waiting for you over there," she said, pointing at the speakers where Kirsty was hiding.

"Hurrah!" the goblin whooped. He jumped up and rushed across the store.

Anxiously, Rachel glanced at Poppy, who was peeping out from behind her hair. Would Kirsty be able to stall the goblin long enough for them to send the piano back to Fairyland?

Goblin Grapple!

Behind the speakers, Kirsty was waiting, her heart thumping. She still hadn't quite decided how to stop the goblin from rushing back to grab the piano when he realised it was all a trick.

But suddenly she spotted a stand holding a microphone that had a long cord attached to it.

Carefully, Kirsty removed the microphone from the stand and took the cord in both hands. Peering round the speakers, she saw the goblin dashing towards her.

Here goes! Kirsty thought.

As the goblin rushed round the side of the speakers, Kirsty was

ready with the microphone cord. Before the goblin realised what was happening, she'd wrapped the cord tightly around him, once, twice, then three times. "Hey!" the goblin

yelled, looking very confused. "Where's Jack Frost?"

"That's what we'd like to know!"
Kirsty replied, whizzing round and round
the goblin several more times until he
was completely wrapped up in the
microphone cord, like a parcel tied
with string.

By this time the goblin realised he'd
been trapped. He shrieked with rage
and tried to free himself, but Kirsty held
on tightly to both ends of the cord.

Suddenly a sweet, melodic tune
filled the air. Kirsty stepped out from
behind the speakers and saw Poppy
flying across the keyboard of her piano.
Dazzling fairy dust fell from her wand
onto the keys, the magic sparkles
making beautiful music.

"Give me my piano!" the goblin squealed furiously. He lunged forwards so forcefully that he pulled the cord from Kirsty's hands. But it was too late. With a final, tinkling melody, the piano vanished in a swirl of fairy magic, and Poppy smiled happily at Rachel and Kirsty.

"Thank you, girls!" she said gratefully.

Looking sulky, the goblin was untangling himself from the microphone cord.

"Does this mean I don't get to be lead singer?" he demanded.

"I'm afraid so," Poppy replied.

The goblin snorted in disgust. "I could have been a mega-star if it weren't for you mean girls!" he muttered as he stomped off.

Poppy laughed. "I hope you'll be able to help the other Music Fairies find their Magical Musical Instruments, girls," she went on, "because a world without music would be no fun at all, would it?"

She waved at Rachel and Kirsty. "Goodbye and good luck!"

"Goodbye, Poppy," the girls chorused as their fairy friend disappeared in a puff of glitter and a swirl of tinkling piano music.

"Poppy's right," Rachel said, gazing round at all the instruments in the store. "The world wouldn't be the same without music."

"Then we have to stop Jack Frost from winning the competition!" Kirsty replied in a determined voice. She grinned at Rachel. "Besides, I don't think the human world is quite ready for Frosty and his Gobolicious Band!"

The Music Fairies

Now Rachel and Kirsty must help

Ellie the Guitar Fairy

Jack Frost has stolen the Music Fairies'
Magical Musical Instruments! Can Kirsty
and Rachel help Ellie the Guitar Fairy to
get her guitar back before Jack Frost wins
the National Talent Competition and puts
Fairyland in terrible danger?

Here's an extract from
Ellie the Guitar Fairy...

Guitar Star!

Rachel Walker smiled across the breakfast table at her best friend, Kirsty Tate. "Yesterday was a really great start to half term, wasn't it?" she said. "I love our holidays together. We always seem to have the best adventures!"

Rachel was staying with Kirsty's family for a whole week over the autumn half term. The two girls had been friends for a long time, and yesterday they had made some new friends – the Music Fairies!

Kirsty nodded. "It was so exciting meeting Poppy the Piano Fairy, and helping her get her Magic Piano back from the goblins. I loved it when–" She broke off suddenly. "Did you just hear something?" she asked.

The two girls sat in silence for a moment, listening. Nobody, not even their parents, knew about their fairy friends, and they were careful to keep it that way. It was their most special secret. The two of them had been to Fairyland many times now, helping all sorts of different fairies and having some very magical adventures.

Kirsty and Rachel could both hear footsteps approaching – and another noise too.

"It sounds like bells," Rachel said in

surprise. "Or a tambourine!" Her eyes
lit up as she turned to Kirsty. "Do you
think it's a musical instrument?"

Yesterday the girls had discovered that
Jack Frost had taken all seven of the
Music Fairies' Magical Musical
Instruments so that he and his goblins
could form a pop group – Frosty and
his Gobolicious Band. Jack Frost was
hoping his band would win the
National Talent Competition that was
being held in Wetherbury at the end
of the week, but the fairies couldn't
let that happen. If he did win, people
would soon find out he wasn't human.
And once the world knew that fairies
really existed, all of Kirsty and Rachel's
magical friends would be in danger
of being discovered by nosy humans!

Kirsty, Rachel and Poppy had managed to find the Magic Piano yesterday, but there were still six other missing Magical Musical Instruments that had to be tracked down...

The Music Fairies

Win Rainbow Magic goodies!

In every book in the Rainbow Magic Music Fairies series (books 64-70) there is a hidden picture of a musical note with a secret letter in it. Find all seven letters and re-arrange them to make a special Music Fairies word, then send it to us. Each month we will put the entries into a draw and select one winner to receive a Rainbow Magic Sparkly T-shirt and Goody Bag!

Send your entry on a postcard to Rainbow Magic Music Fairies Competition, Orchard Books, 338 Euston Road, London NW1 3BH. Australian readers should write to Hachette Children's Books, Level 17/207 Kent Street, Sydney, NSW 2000. New Zealand readers should write to Rainbow Magic Competition, 4 Whetu Place, Mairangi Bay, Auckland, NZ. Don't forget to include your name and address. Only one entry per child. Final draw: 30th September 2009.

Good luck!

Have you checked out the

website at:
www.rainbowmagic.co.uk

Look out for the
Magical Animal Fairies!

ASHLEY
THE DRAGON FAIRY
978-1-40830-349-8

LARA
THE BLACK CAT FAIRY
978-1-40830-350-4

ERIN
THE FIREBIRD FAIRY
978-1-40830-351-1

RIHANNA
THE SEAHORSE FAIRY
978-1-40830-352-8

SOPHIA
THE SNOW SWAN FAIRY
978-1-40830-353-5

LEONA
THE UNICORN FAIRY
978-1-40830-354-2

CAITLIN
THE ICE BEAR FAIRY
978-1-40830-355-9

Available
April 2009